Published by
Armadillo Books
an imprint of
Bookmart Limited
Registered Number 2372865
Trading as Bookmart Limited
Blaby Road
Wigston
Leicestershire LE18 4SE

ISBN 1-84322-166-7

10 9 8 7 6 5 4 3 2

Produced for
Bookmart Limited by
Nicola Baxter
PO Box 215,
Framingham Earl
Norwich NR14 7UR

Designer: Amanda Hawkes
Production designer: Amy Barton

Printed in China

Starting to read – it's perfect!

The not-so-perfect princess in this story helps to make sharing books at home successful and enjoyable. The book can be used in several ways to help beginning readers gain confidence.

You could start by reading the illustrated words at the edge of each lefthand page with your child. Have fun trying to spot the same words in the story itself.

All the words on the righthand page have already been met on the facing page. Help your child to read these by pointing out words and groups of words already met.

Finally, all the illustrated words can be found at the end of the book. Enjoy checking all the words you can both read!

The not so Perfect Princess

Written by Nicola Baxter · Illustrated by Pauline Siewert

ARMADILLO

castle

Princess Pandora has a wonderful castle to live in. She does not like it.

treehouse

branch

crown

Princess Pandora likes her treehouse better.

There is a handy branch to hang her crown on.

Pandora does not like her castle.

dress

Princess Pandora has a
very pretty dress.
She does not like it at all.

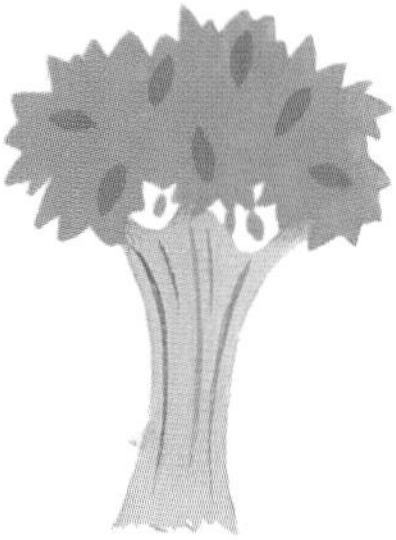

tree

It is no good for
climbing a tree.

It is no good for
splashing in a puddle.

It is no good for jumping
over a gate.

puddle

gate

A pretty dress is no good at all!

bed

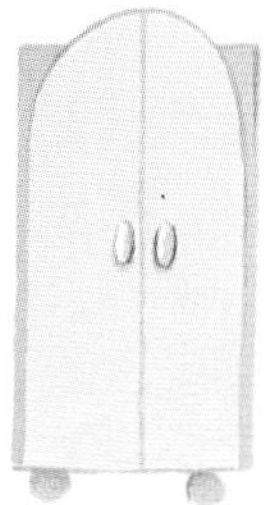

cupboard

toy box

queen

Princess Pandora has a gold crown. She does not like it.

She hides it under her bed.
She hides it in her cupboard.

She hides it
in her toy box.

The queen always
finds it again.

Princess Pandora hides it again!

It is Princess Pandora's birthday. She has lots of presents but…

presents

She does not like her new pink dress.

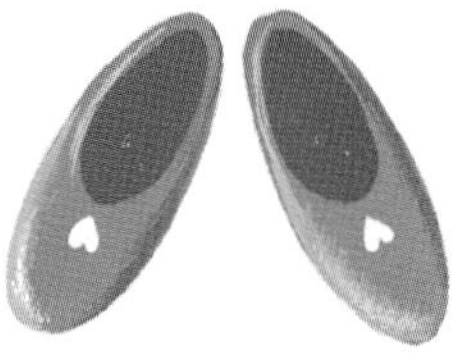

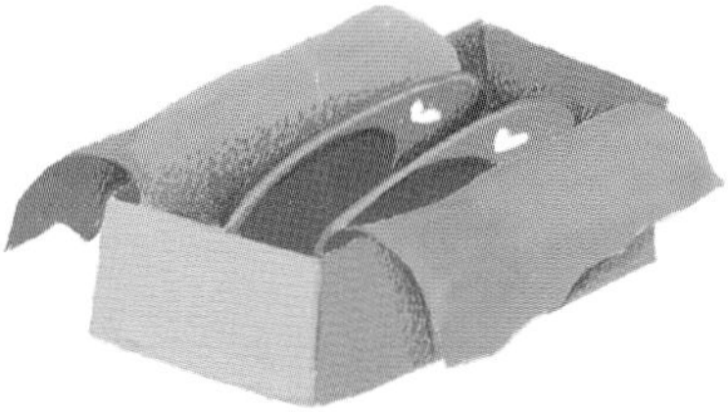

She does not like her new pink shoes.

shoes

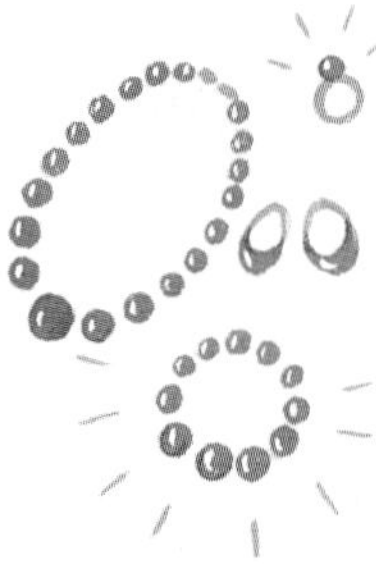

She does not like her new pink jewels.

jewels

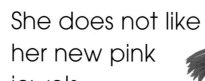

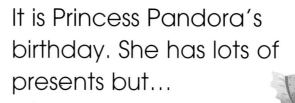

"I want a puppy!" says Princess Pandora.

puppy

There is one more present.

“It is a new puppy!” says Pandora.

Princess Pandora and the
puppy have a wonderful time.

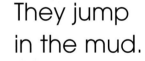

grass

They play
on the grass.

pond

They splash
in the pond.

mud

They jump
in the mud.

flowers

They fall
in the flowers!

They get very, very messy.

They have a wonderful, messy time!

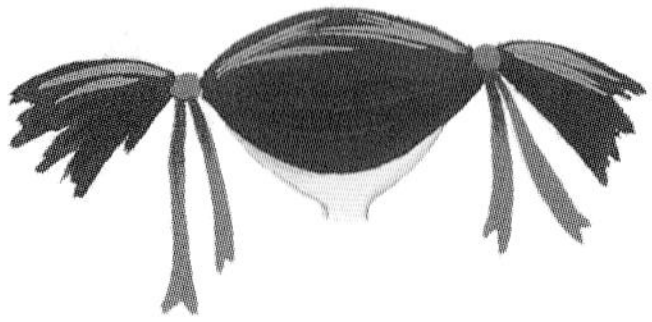

hair

The king and the queen are not happy.

"What happened to our perfect princess?" they ask.

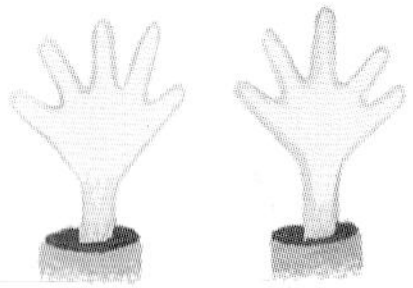

hands

feet

"Look at your hair!
Look at your hands!
Look at your feet!"

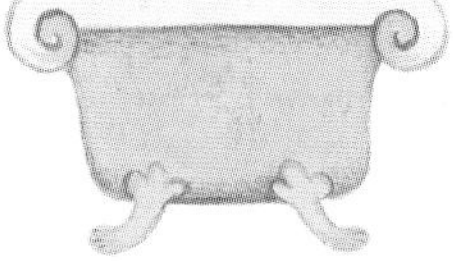

bath

They order the royal bath to be filled!

The princess and the puppy
are not happy.

pillow

nightie

basket

bow

Soon the princess is tucked up in her bed. She is asleep on her royal pillow in her royal nightie.

The puppy is asleep in his basket with a bow on his head.

The king and the queen are happy now.

“Shhh! She is a perfect princess after all,” they say, “when she is asleep!”

Shhh! The perfect princess is asleep.

Picture dictionary

Now you can read these words!

basket

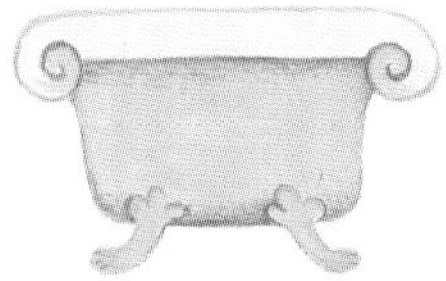

bath

bed

bow

branch

castle

crown

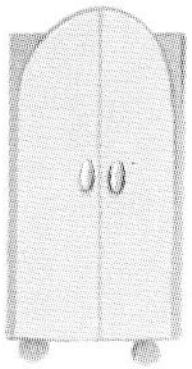

cupboard

dress

feet

flowers

gate

grass

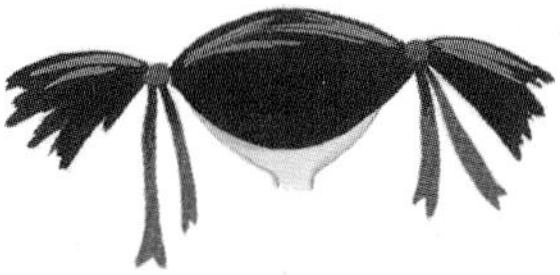

hair

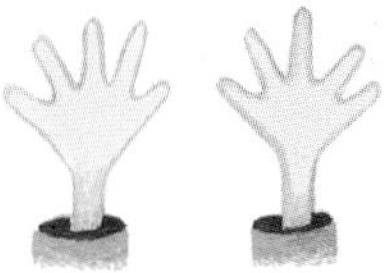

hands

jewels

nightie

mud

pillow

pond

presents

puddle

puppy

queen

shoes

toy box

treehouse

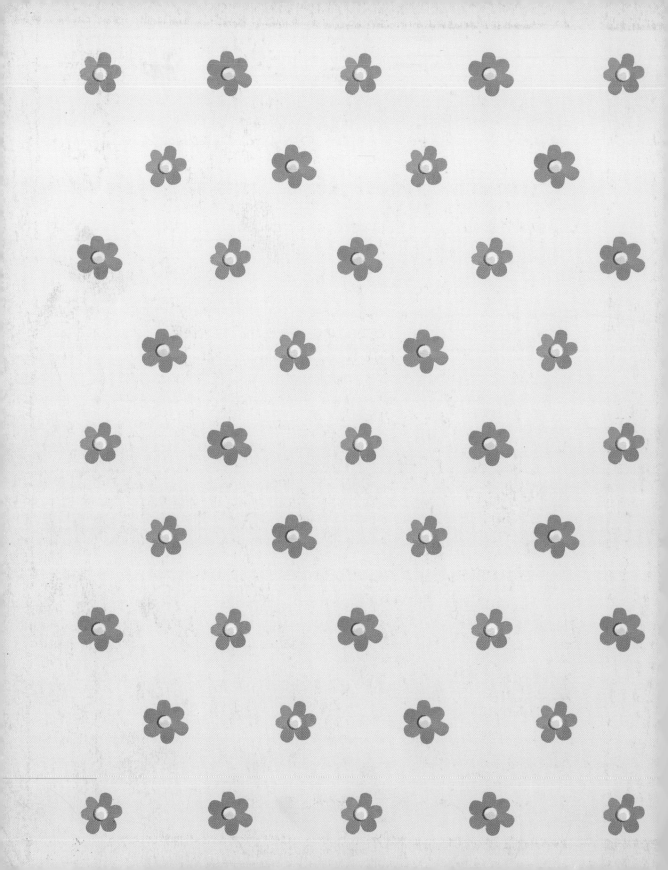